Tyranny in our Times

A novel

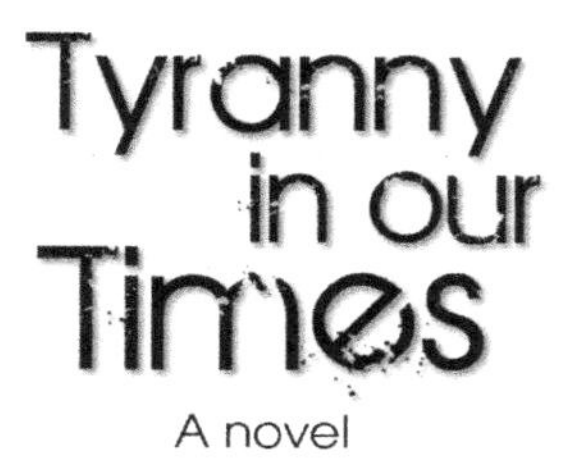

A novel

Brenda Fontaine

TYRANNY IN OUR TIMES

This is a work of fiction. Names, characters, places and incidents either are the product of the author's imagination or are used fictitiously, and any resemblance to actual persons, living or dead, businesses, companies, events, or locales is entirely coincidental.

ISBN: 978-1-4866-0468-5

Word Alive Press
131 Cordite Road, Winnipeg, MB R3W 1S1
www.wordalivepress.ca

Library and Archives Canada Cataloguing in Publication

Fontaine, Brenda, 1947-, author
Tyranny in our times / Brenda Fontaine.

Issued in print and electronic formats.
ISBN 978-1-4866-0468-5 (pbk.).--ISBN 978-1-4866-0469-2 (pdf).--
ISBN 978-1-4866-0470-8 (html).--ISBN 978-1-4866-0471-5 (epub)

I. Title.

PS8611.O56T97 2015 C813'.6 C2014-905689-3
C2014-905690-7

This book is dedicated to my family;
my children, my grandchildren,
and great-grandchildren.

chapter one

Kate Wasko stared at the moon. She stood at her window that cold Saturday afternoon. She was a slightly overweight aboriginal woman with a ponytail. Kate was a teacher at the local Robertson Lake School.

Robertson Lake Reserve had four settlements within its boundary: Willow Creek, Rocky Point, Ross Island, and Robertson Lake itself. Rocky Point faced the forks of the two rivers, Juniper and Mistiko. Mistiko meandered into the interior. Juniper flowed into Robertson Lake.

In between Rocky Point and Willow Creek was a row of houses that stretched out for over a mile. Across from these two was Ross Island, where houses lined the riverbanks. A bridge connected the island to the rest of the community. Groves of trees and boggy areas were interspersed along both shores. Between Willow Creek and Rocky Point, an early years school, Rocky Point Elementary, was situated. The high school stood across the shore of Robertson Lake.

"It's only three in the afternoon and the moon is out," she announced.

"It's winter, after all. The sun will be gone in a couple of hours," her sister, Noela, answered. Noela was visiting for the day from out of town. She lived in Mossy Point, a smaller reserve about eighty miles north.

Noela had just told Kate about the banishment bylaw they had passed in Mossy Point for those who were making trouble in their community. Noela was concerned about her son, who was assaulted by some boys from a gang because they thought he belonged to a rival gang. Her son had in turn gathered some other bigger boys, and they declared war on those who had fought him.

Kate had a way of dealing with bad news or problems. She would focus on something outside or a beautiful object. It seemed to lessen the sting of the pain that came with the news, except now the moon wasn't a thing of beauty, just a distraction and a reinforcement of the cold feeling that crept through her.

"So what's with you and the moon?" asked Noela. "It's always there." She laughed in spite of her problems.

"I never look up. I'm always too busy, with my nose in papers and books. Between teaching and taking the speech course evenings, I've a full plate."

"Why are you taking courses? Haven't you already got your teaching certificate?"

"Yes, but after a few years you're required to take refresher courses. You know I was only a substitute and an educational counsellor in Winnipeg before we moved here."

At that moment the loud crunching of footsteps on snow was heard on the porch steps. Someone was stamping the snow off his or her feet.

The door opened. A cold draft blew in, and a tall heavy-set man in a navy blue parka walked in. The hooded figure carried a box and dumped it on the floor. It was Kate's husband, Carl.

"I brought your box of school stuff in."

"Yes, I had too many bags. Thanks, dear," Kate replied.

Carl pulled off his hood and sneezed. "I'm getting a cold."

The phone rang. It was Jeremy, Kate's brother, asking for money. "Come over and pick it up now before we go out," Kate answered and hung up.

Noela said, "I bought Lotto 649, and when I win, I'm leaving Mossy Point and buying a nice home for my kids."

"Keep dreaming, Noela," Kate said as she poured her sister a cup of coffee.

"Noela says they passed a banishment bylaw at Mossy Point. Don't you think that's illegal?" Kate asked Carl.

"Yes, I think it is. It's against the Canadian constitution." Carl worked at the band office in public works, but he also read up on documents regarding aboriginal and government agreements as well as other government matters. He had taken law courses at the university years before but had to give it up when there was a lack of postsecondary funds to continue his studies. He was planning to go back again.

"Why don't you write something out for me for use?" Noela asked Carl, giving him a serious look.

"Let me do a little research and make a few phone calls this week. I'll need some time."

Yes, of course. I'd like a petition to pass around to get rid of it."

"Yeah, okay," Carl said as he blew his nose. He strolled down the hall and into the bedroom.

There was a quick knock on the door, and Jeremy walked in.

Kate pulled out a bill from her purse and handed it to him.

"Thanks a lot, sis. Much obliged. I'll pay you back next cheque. Sorry, but I'm in a rush," he said and was heading out the door. He turned and waved at Noela as he stepped out the door.

Noela got up, put on her coat, toque and mitts, and announced, "I have shopping to do before I go back. I'll call you later. That's for the listening ear, sis." She was out the door.

Kate picked up the dirty coffee cups, deposited them in the sink, and proceeded to wash them. The phone rang.

"Hi. Are you busy?" It was Angela, a teacher where Kate worked.

"I'm doing some dishes. My sister just left."

"I wanted to ask you what you thought of the meeting on Thursday with the union reps."

"Oh, you mean the one where we were told not to say anything about the system or else we're terminated?"

"Yes, of course. I couldn't believe what I was hearing. Here we pay our union fees, and we're told not to say anything. I always thought they were working for us."

"I guess because they negotiate terms and agreements for us with the division they have a right to talk down to us."

"I know, but I felt like invisible bars of a prison were falling down all around me. It was a weird feeling."

"I suppose we will get use to not saying anything about anything."

"Yes, I've already made up my mind not to. By the way, how is your speech course coming along?"

"It's really fun. I've made two speeches already. I have to make another one for Monday on persuasion."

"Have you decided on a topic?"

"Yes, I've decided to choose a serious topic and not waste my time on trivia. I've chosen abortion."

"Yes, that is a serious one. Are you for it or against it?"

"I'm against it. What kind of a Catholic would I be, to be for it?"

"Catholics do get abortions."

"Not the ones I know."

"Let's leave it at that." Angela paused. "I have to go."

"Okay, I'll see you later."

"Yup." The phone clicked.

Kate went back to her dishes. She was making a hamburger casserole when Carl came out of the bedroom.

"I thought I heard the phone a while ago. Who called?"

"Angela called. She was really concerned about Thursday's meeting."

"Oh yes, the one you were talking about."

"We agreed that it was something we probably have to get used to. It puts critical thinking back a hundred years. Next is the enquiry process. We'll have to blindly accept everything that gets passed on down for the sake of a salary scale. Will we become people without wills or brains? Just think of the stupidity we'll have to accept."

"It's a struggle for power, basically," Carl said as he picked up the telephone. "We ought to tell the girls to come home now. I'll check at my mom's to see if they're there."

"Hello, it's Carl. Are Myra and Molly there? *Why?* Because I want to talk to them. If they're there...What?" He hung up. "Some kid is fooling around with the phone over there." He redialed. He went through the same spiel. He hung up again. "Someone has messed around with her answering machine. A newfangled contraption always gets abused around here."

"What happened?"

"Never mind what happened." He sounded slightly irritated. "I'm going to have to go over there and straighten out that message. Mom doesn't know that they messed around her machine. I'll pick them up."

Edna Wasko was a strong political person in her community and was involved in committees. She was attending one such meeting that evening.

The casserole was done when Carl and the girls got back. Twelve-year-old Molly was giggling when she walked in. Nine-year-old Myra followed with a serious look.

"Molly did it. She was fooling around with the phone," Myra said. "I don't know how to make messages."

"Molly, what did you leave on Granny's answering machine?" Kate asked without taking her eyes off Molly.

Molly puckered up her mouth and rolled her eyes in exasperation. She finally said, "I wasn't planning on leaving it on. I forgot to erase it because the dog went and had a piddle on the floor. I had to wipe it up. We were chasing it around the room. Finally we got him outside. I'm sorry."

"Didn't you hear the phone ringing?"

"Well, I decided to get the dog food to feed him, and then when I didn't see him around outside, I got worried. I went out looking for him, because he isn't supposed to be out too long. He was running down the road. Myra and I were chasing him. We had to yell at some boys up ahead to stop him. We got that stupid dog back, but we got cold."

"Wash up and sit down and eat," Kate said. "You girls will have to stay home while we take Tim to the hockey game. Work on your homework. You still didn't tell me what you left on the answering machine."

"She said, 'Hello, who's calling?' Then she said, 'Why?' and before she hung up she said, 'Baloney,'" Myra declared.

Kate went a little limp with relief. She thought that Molly had used bad language on the phone. She still had to correct her for rudeness. "Molly if anyone had called there it could have made a lot of problems for your granny. That was a rude message. You know that, don't you? Where was Granny?"

"She said something about a meeting before she left," Molly said.

"Sit down and eat," Kate told them.

"I'm not hungry right now," Molly said, and she went down the hall to her room.

chapter two

Kate, Carl and Tim left right after supper. They drove down to Willow Creek to pick another hockey player, Tim's friend Issy. Then they went to the arena. Carl went to help the boys with their skates, and Kate went up to sit in the bleachers. There were other parents milling around and finding seats. Some women sitting a few seats up whose sons were playing on Tim's team were talking rather loudly.

Kate had only lived in Robertson Lake for a few years and still wasn't at ease approaching people. She suddenly felt alone sitting by herself, although she knew Carl would be up shortly. She had gone to Brandon University to get a teaching certificate. Kate had completed her training, but Carl had opted out from his courses in law. Then they went to work in the city for a few years. Kate was a substitute teacher. Life in the city proved to be too hard, and they and their three children came back to Robertson Lake to live permanently. This was Kate's second year teaching elementary school. Before that she had done substitute teaching.

Not long after, Carl came to join her. "I had to stay with the boys until the coach came back. Some of the boys seem to be after Issy, so I stayed to keep the peace. Issy can be easily rattled by words."

Issy, whose real name was Israel, lived his mother, Rose Wood, and his older brother, Rob. Rose was a single mom who had moved to Robertson Lake a couple of years before. Her boys had gotten into trouble because they wanted to fit in so badly. They had gotten involved with the wrong crowd, who often set them up to take the brunt of the gang's illegal activities. Rose had been called to the school a few times for a meeting with the principal. She had sometimes been teary-eyed leaving the school. Kate had felt sorry for her and had been extra soft on the boys.

The teams came out on the ice. The coaches told them to do their warm-ups and then skated around the rink nonstop as their last warm-up exercise.

The game finally started. The Peewees were playing well, but toward the end of the first period Issy bodychecked one of the boys, and the boy fell. He fell, sprawling on the ice.

One of the parents above yelled out to him, "You're not supposed to do that, you stupid kid!"

"I didn't do it on purpose!" Issy yelled back.

"Like hell you didn't," a man's voice boomed out.

Issy was given a penalty for gross misconduct, but as he was skating towards the penalty box, the irate parent yelled out, "Why don't you quit? No one wants you here."

Issy pulled off his glove and made a fist. He yelled, swearing at the parent.

Kate could tell he was hurt. She turned around and looked at the woman indignantly. She said, "You don't have to be mean. He's just a child."

"Why are you sticking up for him? He's a bad kid. They don't belong here. They're nothing but trouble," the woman said vehemently. Her face was white with hatred. She wasn't used to being spoken to like that by another adult.

The coach told Issy to get off the ice for swearing. He was suspended from the game.

Carl said, "That's too bad. I was helping Issy in there, and he was so gung-ho about playing. I think I'll go and calm him down."

Carl followed the crying and frustrated Issy into the dressing room.

The game continued. Tim didn't want to play with his friend being suspended from the game, but eventually he played.

Carl came back up. He said, "Maybe you ought to drive him home and explain things to his mom."

"Yes, I will."

Kate went down to wait for Israel to come from the hallway under the bleachers. He came out, dragging his bag and looking so dismal that it broke Kate's heart. Her stomach tightened as she remembered the woman's words of hate.

"I can drive you home, Israel. Just follow me." Kate preferred to call people by their proper names.

When they arrived at Rose's house, she was at the door waiting. "What happened back there?"

"I was suspended because I fell into a player and they thought I was bodychecking. Then a lady started yelling at me and I swore, I was so mad," Issy said loudly. Just talking about it reopened the unpleasant experience for him. He had been quiet coming home.

"I thought maybe if I put them in hockey he'd be all right. No one would bother him, and he'd have a chance at a normal childhood," Rose's said sadly. Her face turned red with the frustration with the rejection her family was experiencing. Her eyes welled up with tears, and she said angrily, "I wish we hadn't come here, but we're stuck."

"Me, too, I wish I could away from these mean, miserable people," Issy said with anger.

"You'd think coming back to the reserve you'd have some measure of peace," Rose said, wiping a tear off her cheek. "Can you take me to see the woman?"

Kate and Rose went to the arena, and Rose pointed out the woman, who was outside, to her. Rose went up to her and quietly spoke to her. The woman raised her voice and said, "I'm going to phone the police and tell them you assaulted me." She ran inside.

Rose turned back to the car. "Did you hear what she just said?"

"Yes, I did. Don't worry, Rose. I saw everything. You did not assault her. If she does phone the police, tell me and I'll tell them the truth. I'm a witness."

Rose was crying. "You know all I said to her was, 'If you have a problem with my kids, you come and see me. I don't want you to say anything to them.'"

Kate drove Rose home. She felt tired and sad that Mossy Point and Robertson Lake had become hostile and unfriendly places to live in. "My sister, Noela, was visiting me today. She was telling me Mossy Point is getting bad too. They have gangs out there as well. I think it's the drugs that are doing this to them. Her son was assaulted by some boys from a gang."

"I wish there was a place of peace on this earth," Rose said as she wiped her face. She was calming down.

"I'm sure there is."

The car pulled into Rose's driveway, and she got out. "Thanks for everything. I feel better knowing I actually have friendly people around who are helpful."

Kate gave her an encouraging smile. "Okay. See you around."

Rose nodded and walked into the house.

Kate drove away and met a police car driving in the direction of Willow Creek. She swore under her breath. "I can't believe people," she said, whipping her car around and followed the police car back into Willow Creek.

The police car stopped at Rose's. Kate screeched to a stop. She rushed out of the car and met the police as they were walking toward Rose's house.

"Officer," she said, "what is this about?"

"Who are you?" he asked.

"I'm Kate Wasko, and I'm a witness to what happened to Rose. She didn't assault anyone. I was there. She was speaking quietly, trying to tell that woman if she has any problems with her children she should call her, but the woman threatened her right away and told her she was calling you to charge her with assault."

The officer wrote down what Kate was saying. "Okay, but I'll have to let Rose give me her statement."

"Thanks, officer." Kate left, wondering why she had thanked him.

chapter three

The game was over. Tim and Carl were coming out of the arena. Tim had his bag slung over his shoulder. Kate got out. "So, who won?" she said, feigning cheer. She was still feeling the residue of indignation and anger over the treatment of Rose and Israel.

"They did," lamented Tim.

"By how much?" asked Kate.

Tim rolled his eyes and looked at his dad, who said, "They lost to them by four goals. We had two and they had six, but we'll win the next game."

"I don't know if I'll play if Issy is out of the team," protested Tim. "I don't like the way people are at these games."

Carl and Kate looked at each other. Kate felt a weight land on her, and her shoulders slumped.

Carl said, "I don't think he's out of the team. He's just out of the game for tonight and maybe a game or two."

"Issy was so mad he swore," said Tim.

"Yes, and that's why he'd be suspended for a few games," said Carl. "You can't swear, among other things."

"What's the 'other things'?" asked Tim.

"Well, Issy bodychecked, and Peewees aren't suppose to have body contact; that's another serious offence," Carl said.

Tim changed the subject and asked his mom, "Did you take Issy home?"

Kate answered, "Yes, and his mother came to see the woman. I had to drive her, as she doesn't have a car."

Carl asked, "Is everything okay?"

Kate told the story to him. Carl shook his head, especially about the RCMP's involvement. "This is getting really out of hand," he said. "I can't believe the extent some people will go to cause misery and trouble to others."

"You know, the spirit of revenge is a strong motivator for those who plan to do evil," Kate said. She was remembering an incident two years before when a parent had phoned the principal to complain about her behaviour to a student. She was just a substitute then and hardly knew the students.

A couple of students had been playing hockey during indoor recess in the classroom she was in, and their homemade puck hit her in the face. Startled, she grabbed the puck and held it up. She turned around and demanded, "Whose is this?" That was it.

The posture of holding up the puck had been the focus of the parent's complaint. She claimed that Kate had threatened her son.

Months later she found out her next-door neighbour was a friend of the woman who complained. She remembered she had to tell her neighbour a few times that her children were walking away with equipment from her yard; shovels went missing, a toboggan left outside by the door mysteriously disappeared, and old pots for plants were strewn about, some cracked as if rocks had been used to try to smash them. Myra had seen one of the boys take the toboggan, and he wouldn't give it back. He disposed of it somewhere, and it never surfaced again. Finally in anger Kate had told the woman to watch her kids. After that, the incidents seemed to occur more often.

Kate felt there was no sense of justice or integrity in the community. No one cared about correcting their children when they disrespected their neighbours and their property. It was mainly because the kids weren't being supervised. They were just let out, and the kids ruled. Kate knew it was just a matter of time; eventually when they reached a certain age they would break the law, and it would land them in jail. Then it would be a sad day for the parents for not correcting their children's behaviours while they had the opportunity. Sometimes in cooler moments Kate blamed the Youth Offenders Act. Parents could no longer discipline or enforce rules. There was a fine line between discipline and child abuse.

Finally, when Carl and Kate pulled up at their house, Kate said, "I wouldn't be surprised if that woman is related to that woman who complained about me when we first got back here."

"That reminds me, I went to see the manager after you left and told him about the remark the woman made to Issy," Carl said. "He said that he would look into it and talk to the woman."

"Finally! Maybe something will be done about public conduct," said Kate.

As they walked toward the house they noticed the lights were all on. Kate opened the door and was met with a smoke-filled living room. The kitchen area had the heaviest concentration of smoke as it poured out of the oven.

"Oh no!" she exclaimed as she rushed to the stove. Grabbing the oven mitts she opened the oven and saw burnt remains of French fries on a cookie sheet. She pulled out the smoking cookie sheet and rushed to the door. Carl and Tim had left it opened. She flung the whole mess out the door.

Carl strode to the back door and threw it open, letting the smoke out. Then he opened some windows. The smoke seemed to rush out of the house. He grabbed a towel and waved the smoke out the kitchen window.

Kate meanwhile stood outside and looked up at the moon gleaming in its pale light. This smoke seemed like the last straw to the events of the day. Maybe it was the accumulation of all the negativity she experienced that day or maybe recalling that period of her life when rejection became a way of life in Robertson Lake that brought her to the end of her endurance. She burst into tears as she held her head upwards into the star-tossed night and prayed. "This is it. I can't take anymore of this world's hate. If you are a God of love, you either let some flow into this community, or I won't believe you care for us."

She wiped her tears and gulped for some air. She gazed up at the stars and noticed something beginning to shimmer in the sky. She kept on looking at it through her teary eyes and realized northern lights were forming above. They became bright as they flickered with red and yellow hues. In a very short time they became vivid and seemed to dance merrily for a while. Kate realized that her sadness and heaviness were gone. Then she knew that her prayer was answered. God had used the northern lights to dance away her tears. She felt at peace and smiled upward.

"That was fast. Thank you, Lord. You are a God of love, and you love me," she said out loud.

"Come in and see this," Carl said. He went into the girls' bedroom. There they were fast asleep on the bed with the TV on, playing a movie.

Kate woke them up. They groggily opened their eyes. Kate sighed with relief. "Good. You're all right," she said, "But I want you to come and see something."

The girls got up and shuffled out of the room and into the living room.

"Wow, what is that smell and that smoke?" Molly said.

Then she realized and whirled around to look into the oven. Her face dropped. "I'm so, so sorry. I fell asleep waiting for them. Myra was hungry, and I wanted to feed her something. She didn't want the casserole."

"Listen, it was a good thing to try to feed your sister, but never use the oven unless an adult is around to help you. Do you understand? It's very important that you do," Kate said.

"Yes, Mom," Molly said in a contrite voice.

Kate wrapped her arms around her and in a soothing voice said, "I'm just relieved you are all right."

"Yeah, and the house didn't burn down," Carl said. "The house is going to smell smoky for a while, unless we wash down some walls, lickety-split."

Molly perked up and said, "I'll help."

As an afterthought Molly said, "Before you woke me, I was dreaming that I could smell pot. I thought in my sleep, 'Who's smoking so much pot?"

Kate and Carl looked at each other. He shook his head and started closing the windows. Kate picked up a can of aerosol spray and sprayed it around the living room.

"What's pot?" Myra asked Molly.

"Oh, just something I hear the older kids talk about at school," Molly said.

"Do you smoke it?" Myra asked.

"Of course not! Do you think I'm that stupid?" Molly answered, obviously annoyed.

"Pot is another name for marijuana," answered Carl. "It's something that gets a person hooked once they start smoking it. They always want it after. It's addictive. It's a bad and expensive habit."

Kate came out of the laundry room with cleaners and a pail of water. She rolled up her sleeves and said, "Well, let's get cracking." She handed them some rags and dunked her rag into the pail.

chapter four

Later that night when everyone had gone off to bed, Kate snuggled up to Carl. All the walls had been washed down, and Carl had cleaned the ceiling with a sponge mop.

"I forgot to tell you what happened this evening when I was throwing out the cookie sheet with the burnt fries," she whispered.

"What happened?" Carl whispered back.

"I was crying from all the tension from the day. First Noela and her poor son and her worries, then Israel and Rose. I was remembering that woman and her friends who caused so much stress and then this mess we walked into. I couldn't take anymore. I was crying outside. I told God to show me that he's a God of love or else I couldn't believe he cares about us."

"I was wondering why your eyes were red when you came in. Anyway, why wouldn't you believe he cared? Of course he cares."

"I guess at the back of mind I started questioning. It's a complicated thing. You have boundaries to consider. How far do you carry? But that's not the point. I'm trying to tell you what happened out there."

"Oh, sorry. What happened then?" Carl sounded a little exasperated.

"Right away I noticed something starting to move in the sky right above, and it quickly turned into northern lights with flashy splashes of red and yellow. They started to dance really fast. The next thing I knew, I felt all right. I didn't have any tension. I felt peaceful. Isn't it awesome how he used a simple thing like the *wawatew?*"

"Yes, but you love those dancing lights anyway," skeptical Carl said.

"I know, but they never affected me that way before."

"Good night, Kate."

"Good night, Carl."

Kate lay awake for a while thinking about the reality of God's love for her. She felt freshness in her being and contentment that God loved her. Then her thoughts turned to the speech she had to write. She figured that in order for it to be ready for Monday evening's class she would have to work on it tonight. Sunday would not be a good time.

She crept out of bed while Carl snored. Taking her bag of books and writing pad, which contained pages of scribbled notes, she tiptoed into the kitchen and spread them out on the table. She reread the underlined passages in the history book about human sacrifices and empires that fell and the excerpt of Roe versus Wade in the book of law and cases. She reread the articles on the abortion statistics, its history, and the arguments for and against it.

Kate noted that there were no absolutes in the arguments for those who were pro-choice. You couldn't nail anything down to a concrete position. Every argument seemed to slither in and out. No matter how you looked at it, pro-choice was based on the matter of convenience, even when adoption was a reasonable avenue for the single mom and other women who weren't ready for a baby.

Those who defended life for the unborn took staunch positions on an absolute to argue for the survival of the child.

She prayed, "Lord, you already came through for me tonight. I have to ask you to help me again. I've got to write this speech for my class. I need a conclusion, and if you want to give one, I'd sure appreciate it. Thanks, God. Oh yes, forgive me for swearing earlier this evening. I was angry at what was happening to Rose and Israel. Please look after them. In Jesus' name, amen."

Kate sat back and stared at the work in front of her. In her mind a line appeared. It had a distinct beginning and an end. "Why am I seeing a line?" she whispered to herself. The thought came, *Forty years of grace as those in the past got.* Then a darker line started at the beginning and rested well past the middle of the line and looked like it covered three-quarters of the original line. "What is that then?" she thought. Another thought came. *Forty years of grace has begun and is almost finished. The forty years is opportunity for repentance; then the earth will revolt against the crimes against the unborn and the sins of immorality.*

Kate quickly wrote it down. Then she wrote her speech and was finished in a short while, or so it seemed. She rubbed her eyes and looked at the clock. It was well past two o'clock.

She wondered what would happen after the forty years of grace were over. She dared not ask. She closed her books and gathered up her papers. Shutting off the lights, she left the room and crept down the hall to her bedroom, but sleep eluded her and she tossed around. Her thoughts were tumbling over issues and events of the past few days. She worried that Molly was being exposed to the unsavoury conversations at school. She knew there was a lot swearing among the students, and her children heard it every day. She had to speak to Molly and Myra about it. Finally, exhausted, she fell asleep.

She woke up late the next morning. The sounds of clanging pots and pans and slamming of cupboard doors woke her up.

Putting on her bathrobe, she went into the kitchen. Carl was cooking breakfast.

"Coffee smells good," Kate said.

"You sure slept a lot," Carl said.

"I got up to write my speech after you fell asleep, and it's ready for tomorrow's class."

"Have some of my cooking, my night owl woman."

Kate poured coffee for both of them and set the table. "The house smells okay," she said. "Looks and smells like we did a good job last night."

The phone rang. It was Rose. She sounded upset. "Some kids threw rocks at my windows last night and broke two. The boys couldn't sleep for the rest of the night, and I had to stay up and watch the house."

"Did you phone the band constables?"

"Yes, but they can't do too much. They said they'll do a surveillance of the area."

"Yeah, they're not armed, not even with a club. Do you know the boys who broke your windows?"

"Issy recognized a couple of them. I told the band constables."

"They'll probably get picked up for questioning."

"It's a nerve-racking experience to have this happen in the middle of the night."

"Yes, it must be."

"Issy says he wants to leave Robertson Lake."

"Yes, I heard him last night."

"I have to start planning how I'm going to move and where."

"I'm really sorry that you're going through so much harassment. Let me know what happens."

"Okay, I sure will." They hung up.

Carl said, "Trouble in Willow Creek again?"

Kate told him Rose's story.

Carl shook his head. "If only parents would care what their children are doing and stop believing their lies. They always blame their victims, too."

Kate glanced at the clock. It was going onto eleven o'clock. She remembered that Mass would be beginning then. She hadn't been to church in months.

"I think I'll go to church this morning," she announced. "Where are the girls?"

"Still sleeping, I think," Carl responded.

"I'd like to take them, but there isn't much time. Next Sunday I'll take them for sure. Things are getting too chaotic around here. It's time to get back to the basics and to sanity. I don't suppose you'd want to come."

"Don't even try. You know how I feel about church and priests," Carl said.

Carl's father had been in a residential school and had a bad experience. As soon as he was able to leave, he never went to church again. Carl's opinion had a second-hand motive. It was never discussed.

"After last night I think I ought to go. First with the wawatew, and then when I was writing I actually saw a timeline in my head when I was praying for guidance for my conclusion. And the thoughts I was receiving were unusual. It looks like we go will through something in the near future because of the millions of abortions and the immorality that's going on in the world. The earth will revolt against the sins of our generation."

Carl was silent. He was dumbstruck. He hadn't expected to hear that from Kate. He cleared his throat and said, "I hope you don't go around saying that. I don't want people to think you've fallen off your rocker. You better keep quiet about that." He frowned, with deep furrows on his forehead. His worry over Kate was obvious.

Kate was quiet. She was disappointed at Carl's reaction. When she didn't say anything, Carl asked her, "Are you going to tell anyone?"

"I'll have to think about it," she said. "It does make a fitting conclusion."

"Don't you care what people will think?"

"Carl, I'm surprised that you actually care what people think. What people are you concerned about? The ones who are causing a lot of trouble for others? Do you really care what they think? I don't. If it's a matter of pride, I don't think I have any left, after what I've been through and seen and heard. Sorry, but I think my time is up on the fence. I can't sit there anymore. Don't worry so much."

"I didn't think I'd have a doomsday prophet for a wife," Carl replied.

chapter five

Kate sat through the Mass, listening intently and participating as well as she could. She paid close attention to the readings. Normally her mind would drift into other things when the Scriptures were read or the sermon was preached. She prayed the Apostles' Creed as loudly as she thought was socially permissible. She laughed inwardly when the children in front of her turned around to look at her. Finally, the moment she was waiting for. The priest, Father James, got up to give the sermon.

Kate was searching for something special, and she listened with great expectation. She felt that God wanted her to hear something important that had to do with her whole life, because she felt a change was taking place at last. She was somewhat disappointed when the priest taught on forgiveness. However, it stuck in her mind when he said, "You will be overwhelmed by the stress or problems of life if you are carrying grudges or if you haven't forgiven others. You will be free of a burden when you forgive and surrender everything into Jesus' care."

Kate thought hard into her past about all the people who had aggravated her and those whom she didn't like. She realized that the list in her head was starting to get long. She mentally resolved that she would forgive each person, one by one. When she came to her neighbour's kids stealing from her and their dogs coming to piddle on her deck, it caused a major struggle within her. She had wished to move away from them so many times.

At least I got those others out of the way, she thought. *I'll do this one when I see them today.*

She went home happier. She felt that she had accomplished something. As she drove she sang one of hymns from the service.

She stopped at the gas station. As she got out of her car, she saw Issy surrounded by some boys on the road. He was carrying a bag of groceries.

The gas attendant came out.

"Ten dollars, please," Kate said, but her eyes reverted back to the group of boys. She waited as the gas attendant poured the gas into her tank. Kate dug into her purse, pulled out a ten, and handed it to the attendant.

"I don't have time to go in and pay. I'll come back later to sign the sheet," she said. She motioned to the group of boys. "I have to rescue that one," she said.

"Oh, him. He was chased by here. It would help if he didn't swear at them. Maybe they'd leave him alone."

"I think one of those boys is a hockey player he knocked down on the ice," she said.

One of the bigger boys landed a punch on Issy's arm. Another one jumped in and punched him in the face. Issy yelled out in pain.

"Leave him alone, you bullies!" Kate hollered. She got in, pulled out of the gas station, and honked her horn at the boys. She rolled down her window and yelled, "Get in, Israel. Your mom wants you to go home."

The boys ran away to the other side of the road and through a path in the snow.

Issy came to the car. "I almost threw my bag of food away to run away," he said. "Thanks, Mrs. Wasko, for stopping to pick me up." His young frame was visibly shaking. He rubbed his face. "I got punched on my arm and my face."

"Yes, I saw them," Kate said, "We'll tell your mom, and we can phone the police from your place." She headed toward Willow Creek.

"I don't want her to phone the police. They just do worse things when you do."

"The police won't allow them to keep on harassing you. Who are those other boys? I still don't know all these kids out here."

"They belong to the gang I used to belong to, but I don't want to hang out with them anymore. They're threatening me now for quitting."

In a few minutes they were in Willow Creek. "Do you want me to go in with you?"

"No, it's okay. I'm all right now. I'll tell her myself."

There was a sad resignation and dead calm about Issy that worried Kate. "Tell your mom. The police are not going to let them get away with it if they're reported. Tell your mom to call me, Issy."

Kate dropped him off. She turned around and drove home wondering about him. She couldn't help feeling Issy was giving up on life but hoped it was just a temporary reaction to the assault by the boys.

"I can't let this go without trying to help them," Kate said to herself. She swung her car around on the road, swerving wildly and narrowly missing the ditch. "Whoa, there," she yelled. She headed back to Willow Creek.

Next thing she knew a police siren rang out loud and shrill behind her. "Oh, heck, where did he come from?" she said. She pulled to the side of the road. The police officer got out and came to the side of her window. She rolled down her window and smiled.

"How much have you had to drink?" he asked her as he peered at her face intently and sternly.

Kate bit her lip to keep from laughing. The smile on her face told him she wasn't taking him seriously. "Do you realize that you almost ended up in the ditch making that U-turn? You drove like an inebriated person."

"I'm sorry, officer. I haven't had anything to drink. I was in a hurry to get back home. It's Sunday, and I just came back from church when I saw Israel Wood being surrounded and punched by a group of boys. I just dropped him off at home. He didn't want us to tell you, because he thinks they will do something worse to him. He quit their gang, and now they're harassing him. I was turning back to convince him to let us phone you. I was worried about his mood. I wouldn't want him to do something that would end up bad or even tragic. Even adults were after him last night at the arena. I can't imagine how anyone can feel anything but paranoia after this."

"You've done your part. Let us go and talk to him," the officer said, "and I'm letting you off this time with a warning. Drive safely."

"Yes, and thanks, officer," Kate said. The officer went back to this cruiser and drove off into Willow Creek.

"Why so glum? Aren't you supposed to be full of peace coming from church?" Carl chided as she walked in.

"The church was great and peaceful, but the devil sure gets busy bursting bubbles," Kate said.

"Why? What happened to burst your bubble?" Carl asked.

Kate recounted everything that happened the past hour on her way home.

"I don't understand why you had to make such a sharp turn in the middle of the road," Carl said.

"I was in a hurry to get home, but I had to go make sure

that Rose and Issy would phone the police."

"Okay, you did your good deed for the day, so why so down in the dumps?"

"I realized at some point between here and there that we are facing a huge problem that seems to get bigger. We have to do something. I can't understand why these preachers on the radio don't preach about respect, love, and being just."

Carl wrapped his arms around Kate. "Kate, I know you. Once you set your mind on something, you'll see it through."

Kate's smile was one that came from within and washed over her like a warm wave.

"By the way, Jeremy called while you were gone. He got picked up for being drunk early this morning. He was thrown into the tank, but they're letting him go now. He wants a ride."

"No, he'll have to walk or hitchhike. It isn't that far."

Myra piped up, "Jeremy's in a tank? I only know of gas tanks. What's a 'tank'?"

Kate answered, "It's a place where people are taken when they're found wandering on the road, drunk. The police take them to the jail and put them in a cell for a few hours until they're not drunk anymore. Otherwise they could fall, pass out, and freeze to death. It's for their own good."

"Okay, got it." Myra said. "Stupid Jeremy," she muttered.

chapter six

Monday rolled in with the sun shining. Kate was back at work, but she noticed a subdued atmosphere in the school. The teachers weren't sitting around in the staff room drinking coffee like they usually did for a few minutes each morning. Some got caught up on the latest news. There would be cheerful chatter and laughter. Now, they were all in their classrooms attending to their tasks.

Kate met a couple of them, who seemed to be in a world of their own. She knew it was due to last week's meeting.

She decided to send out a feeler when she met Mr. Thompson, a tenth grade teacher, heading towards the doors. He had dropped off his son in grade one. She asked him, "How are you today?"

He had a wistful look and replied, "As well as I can be, under the circumstances."

"There seems to be a low morale this morning," Kate said.

"I think it's going to stay that way for quite a while."

His gait quickened as he walked out like a flitting shadow.

Kate decided that the less she said, the better. She decided then that she would not say anything about it anymore to anyone.

"I'm not going to stir that cauldron of misery," she said to herself. "If I were to do something about it, it would probably end up in a puddle of something awful. Who said, 'If a thing is worth doing, it's worth doing badly'? Carl knows, I'm sure."

Kate spent the rest of her day in the classroom and was too busy to think about it any further. It was like an oasis of forgetfulness.

That didn't last. When she got to her car after work, she noticed scratches on the driver's door. Someone had scratched a swear word on it. She knew it was one of the boys who assaulted Issy and she had yelled at.

Another teacher was walking by to her car. "Hey, check this out," Kate said. She pointed out the swear word to her. "This is for rescuing Issy Wood yesterday when some boys surrounded him and were punching him."

"Isn't it terrible?" the teacher said, "And the worst thing is, the parents believe those boys and stick up for them. It's just a vicious cycle."

"I wonder if adults would do something like that," Kate said. "A parent went after Issy at the arena this weekend, and I stuck up for him. They were brutal. The kid left the rink in tears."

"That Issy is really getting it, isn't he?"

"And anyone else who defends him."

"So what are you going to do about this?"

"Since I didn't see who did it, I can't charge anyone. I think it's time to relocate. I mean, a group of people should move to another area where they can live in peace and not have to face the hassle of dealing with hate mongering."

"How are you going to do that? That's a big task. I think they tried to years ago."

"Indian Affairs probably said 'no' to that one."

"And I think you have to use a different reason besides leaving hate mongering. Something like, the physical terrain is muskeg and rocks and you want drier, better ground."

"That's a good one. Okay."

"Let me know how it goes." The teacher chuckled and was gone.

Kate felt better with that spark of hope. Maybe there was something that could be done. She prayed under her breath, "God, help me." She drove home in a better spirit.

Later that evening at her speech class her serenity was overcome by nervousness at the prospect in delivering her speech. She had decided to entitle it "Changes Have a Ripple Effect."

Her turn came up, and she cleared her throat and began.

"Ladies and gentlemen, My topic for this evening is about Marxist feminists and the issues of abortion and related topics. I speak from my convictions about life. Although there are many arguments for and against abortion, we still can make the right choice on where we stand if we just stick to the basics of our core values. If we do legislate the right to abort here, it will cause a major shift in change, and not for the better. It will affect the disabled and terminally ill, and euthanasia will be legalized.

"The court case of Roe versus Wade in 1973 opened up abortion in the United States. The Supreme Court ruled that a woman along with her doctor could decide to terminate a pregnancy in the first trimester. In the second trimester, only if the woman's health was in danger could her pregnancy be aborted.

"Open the door an inch to the devil, and he kicks the door wide open. Today pregnancies are being terminated in the third trimester, almost when the baby is ready to leave the womb. The womb is an unsafe place for our children because the laws have made it unsafe. That is why we need to fight this leading and paramount issue of abortion. It is the one that carries the clout, so to speak, in our decline as a society.

"Historically, abortion always has been a deep, dark, clandestine secret of those who ended pregnancy. In the Victorian era it was a disgrace to become pregnant without being married, and so it was done in secret. Some died in the process. Some were never able to have children again. This is the basis used by the pro-abortion groups to achieve their right to abortion.

"The feminist group has fought for the right to terminate pregnancy. Not too much has changed in the attitudes toward it. Many women have ended their pregnancies through abortion, in the millions around the world, although it still is considered an act that is immoral in itself. If it were okay, there would be no sense of guilt, but because it isn't okay, the guilt remains.

"If we were to examine the history of civilizations of the past and the empires that rose and fell, we could come across many instances of humans, particularly children, used as sacrifices on altars to appease their angry gods. The Aztec Empire fell as a result of human sacrifice. The Roman Empire fell for more than one reason, but the main one was homosexuality. I believe these nations were given enough time and warnings to stop their atrocities of shedding human blood, just like the Hebrews were given time in the desert to get rid of their idolatry. They wandered in the desert for forty years. They received warnings, but time and time again they went back to their old ways of doubting and complaining.

"I believe we are within the range of those forty years of our time, and our North American empire will fall along with those nations that perform these abnormal practices. We have begun to see massive changes in weather patterns and we will begin to experience problems with water and earthquakes breaking out in different parts of the world. Volcanoes erupt. The earth can no longer stand us and our atrocities. Although everything is explained through science and environmental studies, the fact remains that we have become a corrupt generation through the new laws.

"Today we demand so much freedom and liberalism that we actually have less of it as we go farther. We can divert the course of things. We can make a difference. We don't have to remain corrupt if we go back to biblical truths. We can begin with preserving the sanctity of life by fighting abortion and asking them to rescind the same-sex marriage legislation. Otherwise, we are doomed. Let's not forget Sodom and Gomorrah.

"If we don't spend too much time arguing over the right religion we can get together and attack these impending changes. We still have the time to make a difference and stop the spiral downward decline of our society. Write letters to our government. Maybe do protest marches, but let's do something. Last but not least, pray."

Kate sat down with her heart pounding. She felt that all eyes were on her. She was afraid that there would be a backlash from the professor. Her mouth felt dry. She grabbed her bottle of water and gulped some down.

The professor cleared his throat and said, "That was a speech of persuasion."

Everyone clapped. It was as if they had been waiting for his approval before they could clap, Kate thought.

A couple of them came up to her after and commented. "I agree with what you said. I think it is a good speech. Use it again somewhere."

Another one said, "I don't think it's because of these issues that we are having a problem with weather and earthquakes, but to each his own."

Kate realized that you can't convince everyone, but you may manage to convince a few.

She went home deep into her thoughts.

As soon as she walked in, Carl said, "Noela called. She wants you to call her ASAP."

Kate went to the phone.

Noela answered, "Yes, Kate, I called. I have some bad news to tell you."

Kate braced herself against the counter. "What's the matter?" she whispered.

Carl was studying her face.

"The council decided that they would banish some families from Mossy Point, and we're one of them. We have two weeks to find a place and move out."

"Oh no! We'll help you," Kate said.

Carl went into the bedroom.

"So I'm going to go ahead to Winnipeg and look for a place. I need you to look after the kids while I go, and I'll be back in a week hopefully. Then I'll come and pack up."

"Okay, sure," Kate said.

Carl came out and held up some papers.

"What is it?" Kate asked.

"I wrote out a petition today, and we can go and drop it off tonight if she wants."

"Did you hear that?" Kate asked Noela.

"I sure did," Noela said.

"Okay, we'll see you then. Bye."

chapter seven

Carl left to go and gas up for the drive to Mossy Point. Kate phoned a babysitter as soon as he left. One of the girls from neighbours down the hill was willing to come. Kate made a thermos full of tea, and as soon as Carl was ready they left.

Their car rumbled along on the snow-packed road. They slipped past the houses under the streetlights, past the dump at the edge of town and into the dark night. The overcast sky made the night a little darker as they left Robertson Lake.

They listened to the radio for a while. After half an hour of driving, they had just crossed the bridge across the creek. Their car lights shone on a tall figure ahead with a knapsack. His face was covered with a balaclava that was frosted around the mouth. He held out his arm with his thumb sticking up, indicating he wanted a ride.

Carl slowed down the car. "Who's this?" he asked Kate.

Kate responded, "I have no idea."

The man got in at the back. His muffled "Thank you" came in a gentle voice.

Carl and Kate felt at ease right away. Kate thought she heard tiny chimes tingling as the man spoke.

"Where are you heading?" Carl asked.

The man mentioned a town to the east.

"We can take you as far as Mossy Point, because that's as far as we're going," Carl said cheerfully.

"Any distance is fine with me," he answered. "By the way, my name is Jesse Christianson. What's yours?"

"I'm Carl Wasko, and that there is Kate, my better half," Carl responded heartily.

Kate turned to look at Jesse and gasped. Jesse had taken off his balaclava, and his face was marred with red gashes across his forehead. One eye seemed smaller than the other.

"I'm sorry. I didn't mean to gasp. I thought I'd recognize you. Your name does ring a bell, but I don't think I've seen you before."

"I don't usually go out in public much. I was down to visit friends for a short time."

"Would you like some tea?" Kate asked as she poured some out into her thermos cup. "That's some walk you just made. You must be thirsty." She reached to the back with her cup.

Jesse took it almost reverently. He held it in his hands for a few seconds, then slowly drank it. Kate wondered why his actions seemed so familiar.

"Ah, this is so good, so nice and warm," Jesse finally said. "Thanks so very much."

Again Kate seemed to hear tiny chimes tingling. She shook her head and dismissed it. "I can give you more. My sister Noela usually gives us something to drink when we visit her," Kate said.

"Did you say your name is Kate Wasko?" Jesse asked.

"Well, Carl did. Yes, I am Kate Wasko."

"One of my friends' daughters was telling me about a speech you made this evening," said Jesse. "She was worried about it."

"But I just made that speech about just about an hour ago, and we picked you up way out here," Kate said. "Do you have a cellphone?"

"Why yes, I do," Jesse said, sipping at his tea, "but right now, we're out of the service area."

"Well, that explains things. Why was she worried?" Kate knew why, but she wanted to know if it was what she thought it was.

"Given that many things are happening in the world, she can't help but agree that it's because of abortion and other immoral things that are causing our decline, as you put it. She worries. She confessed that she had an abortion last year and has felt guilty about it since."

"Wow, I didn't know that," Kate said, "but there is forgiveness if she repents and doesn't do it again." Kate wondered where the words were coming from. She poured another cup of tea when Jesse handed back the cup.

"Yes, I told her that if she confesses her sin and asks forgiveness, she will receive forgiveness."

Kate was relieved.

Carl said, "So you gave the doomsday message," shaking his head.

"I had a strong feeling I had to give it," Kate said. "Say, are you Catholic?" she asked Jesse.

"No, but she is."

"Kate, do you have ask such personal questions?" Carl remonstrated.

"Hmm, I wonder if Angela knows her," Kate said, ignoring Carl.

"Yes, she does," Jesse said, "and it's okay, Carl. I don't consider it personal."

"That explains Angela's strange comment about Catholics and abortions the other night."

Carl said, "We're almost at the junction going into Mossy Point, Jesse."

"I appreciate the ride. I'm sure someone will be coming shortly," Jesse said as he was handing the cup back.

"Have a safe journey. Here, I'm sure this will come in handy on your way home," Carl said as he handed Jesse a twenty dollar bill.

Jesse smiled. The gashes on his head seem to diminish as he took the bill. "Thank you. As for you, Kate, you're on the right track. If more people would turn away from wickedness, the world would be a better place to live in," Jesse said as he got out.

He gave a little wave as they pulled into the intersection and drove on. A minute later Kate noticed his knapsack sitting on the back seat. She looked behind, but the clouds of snow made by the car made it impossible to see where they had dropped him off.

"Hey, Carl, did you bring a knapsack, or is that Jesse's?"

Carl came to sudden halt. He peered into the back.

"Oh, no. Let's catch him before he gets picked up." He swung the car around, backed up, and drove forward and back again. They finally drove back to where they dropped him off, but Jesse was nowhere in sight. They drove in the direction he was heading, thinking they'd see him a few yards ahead or the taillights of a car ahead. They continued like that, with Carl picking up speed and driving faster, but to no avail. Jesse had simply vanished.

They turned around on a straight stretch of road and headed back to Mossy Point. Neither one said a word for a while.

Finally Carl spoke. "It just seems like we had a visitor from another world."

"Yes," Kate said. "Did you see the gashes around his head? They're old wounds, but you can see them."

"What are you saying? We picked up Jesus tonight?" Carl said incredulously.

"Didn't you notice how peaceful it felt when he got in?" Kate asked.

"He had a very good vibe," Carl said. "I liked him right away."

"Yeah, and we weren't afraid of him or nervous at all." Kate's words tumbled out.

"I feel refreshed, like I've just got a good rest," Carl continued.

"I feel happy, bottom line," Kate said. "I think we could say he was sent, maybe an angel in disguise. Who are we, anyway, that Jesus would come and pay us a visit? We're just a couple of natives bumbling around down here. I think he's an angel."

"Yeah, maybe it's better to say that," Carl said reluctantly. "We should check out his backpack to see if there's a wallet with an address in there."

Kate leaned back and retrieved the knapsack from the back seat. She felt a warmth spread over her as she held it in her lap. "It feels rather light," she remarked. She took a deep breath and unzipped the bag.

There near the bottom lay a black book on top of some clothing. Kate pulled it out and held a Bible in her hand.

"Look, this plus a few pieces of clothing is all there is."

Kate opened up the Bible where a piece of paper was sticking out. There on the paper was written the sinner's prayer and at the bottom a Bible verse. "'My yoke is easy and my burden is light.' This is for you. Read it and grow in the knowledge and wisdom of God."

Kate handed the note to Carl. "Here, read this."

Carl had slowed down and took the note and read it. He nodded and tucked the note into his shirt pocket. He took the Bible and examined it.

"You have a Bible. Do you mind if I keep this one?" he asked. "I don't think Jesse will mind. Where did he say he was going?"

Kate drew a blank. She couldn't remember. After a moment she said, "I forget."

They were pulling into Mossy Point. They got out and saw the lights were on at Noela's house. Grabbing the brown envelope with the petition inside, Carl strode with a lively step to the door. Kate felt light on her feet as she walked toward Noela's.

Knocking on the door, they heard Noela's voice telling them to come in. "What took you people so long? It's past eleven. I thought you got into an accident or ran into the snowbanks," Noela chided.

"We picked up a hitchhiker between here and Robertson Lake and dropped him off at the junction. Then we noticed he left behind his knapsack, and we had to go back to try to find him. We went about five kilometers past the junction trying to catch up to him, but there was no sign of him," Kate said.

"Wow, you picked up a man who mysteriously disappeared," Noela said.

Carl handed the brown envelope to Noela, who eagerly opened it and read. "This is good. I'll make a couple of copies for the other parents, and we'll get enough names. Thanks very much."

After drinking a cup of coffee Kate and Carl said they had to go. After a few minutes they left and returned to Robertson Lake, unaware that Noela was on the phone telling her friends about the Waskos' mysterious passenger.

For every small community, news like this is a welcome relief to its humdrum life.

chapter eight

As they drove into Robertson Lake, Kate and Carl saw a fire truck pass them going toward Willow Creek.

A cold feeling settled into Kate's chest as she watched it go. "Let's follow the fire truck," she said.

"It's late," Carl replied.

"I know, but look where it's heading."

"Okay, but don't get too involved. We've done our good deed for the day," said Carl resignedly.

They drove quietly to Willow Creek as the fire truck headed straight toward billowing smoke.

"Smoke is coming from Rose's house," Kate said.

They pulled up behind the fire truck, and the firemen hurriedly unraveled the hoses from the truck.

Kate and Carl stepped out their car. Rose was running out of the house with smoke trailing behind her. She carried an armload of blankets. Her boys stood close to the door, staring into the house. Their television was beside them, and they each held some clothes.

One of the firemen ran toward the family and ushered them away from the house and onto the road.

Kate yelled, "Over here."

Rose and the boys came toward them, and Kate saw that they had tears running down their faces.

"We came home a little while ago and saw there was a fire in the kitchen and a broken window. We phoned the emergency unit, and they got the fire truck for us. The boys were trying to put out the fire at first, but it was already spreading to the ceiling, so we each grabbed something and came out."

There was a group of people standing off to the side watching the flames lick the interior of the walls. The firemen aimed the spouts of water at the roof and flames in the kitchen. Rose and her boys sat huddled in the car, staring at their burning house. Rose sat with a sad, faraway look in her eyes. Finally she asked, "Can you take the boys to my grandmother's trailer with this stuff? I'll go later when I can find a ride for the rest of the stuff I'll try to save, although the furniture will probably be wet and smoky."

Carl got out and opened the trunk. He grabbed the TV sitting in the snow, heaved it into the trunk, and carefully lowered the lid over it.

"Okay, we'll take the boys to your grandma's and come and check on you."

Kate and Carl drove the boys towards Rocky Point.

"How long were you gone from the house?" asked Kate.

"We went to Grandma's for supper, and we stayed to visit her for a while, watching a movie. Then we walked home," Rob answered.

"Yeah, it's kind of a long walk," Issy joined in.

"How did the window get broken?" asked Kate.

"I guess someone broke it while we were gone," said Issy.

"I can take a good guess who would break it," said Rob.

"It doesn't matter anymore, because we're going to leave anyway," Issy said, "but I feel lonely for my house."

"The same persons who broke the window probably started the fire," Kate said.

"And they said I was bad," said Issy, "I wouldn't do that to a person, to set fire to their house."

Finally they pulled up the driveway of their grandmother's trailer. They unloaded their belongings, and Carl got out the TV and took it in.

The boys explained to their grandmother what happened, and she gave a cry of disbelief at their plight. "Oh no. A fire! That's terrible."

Carl spoke to her. He walked back to the car and got in.

Kate asked, "What did you say to her?"

"I told her Rose was still at the scene and we would go and help her out."

They left Rocky Point in a state of unbelief at what was happening to Rose and her family. Kate looked at her watch. It was one o'clock. "It's pretty late. I don't know what shape we'll be in for work tomorrow, but I guess we'd better see what we can do."

A police car drove away from Willow Creek as they neared it.

When they arrived, the fire was out. The house was saturated with water, dripping on all sides.

The firemen were walking in with their flashlights. They surveyed the black, sodden interior. Rose stood shivering on the road. Her tired face spoke volumes. Kate's heart went out to her.

"The police were here and wanted a statement," Rose said. "I told them tomorrow would be a better time. I'm too shocked and tired to talk to anyone. I'm ready to collapse. Can you take me home?" Rose was shaking. "I mean, to my grandma's. I forgot. I no longer have a home." Her voice cracked under the strain of the night.

"Of course we can," Kate said.

They drove quietly all the way back to Rocky Point.

Finally Rose said, "I don't care to save anything. I just want to get away from here."

chapter nine

The next day, Kate was tired, and the strain of having to get to work was heavy. The memory of the night before was still fresh. She worried about Rose's state of mind and hoped that a good night's sleep would improve her outlook a bit.

She saw that the principal's office was opened. She walked in. He was sitting at his desk writing.

"Excuse me. I guess you know that Rose Wood's house burnt late night and that her boys will probably not be in today," Kate said.

"That's too bad. I'm sorry to hear that. Yes, they'll be excused. It's not their fault, after all. I'll let their teachers know."

Kate walked to her classroom. The quietness brought memories of other problems. She realized that the restrictions imposed by their union didn't seem to bother her, not after what happened last night. That demoralizing spirit had left. At least it had for Kate.

The next few days flew by. Kate developed an avid interest in reading the Bible. Carl would disappear into their bedroom, and Kate caught him reading the Bible from Jesse's knapsack.

On Thursday, Kate's thoughts turned to Noela and the petition. She phoned her after work. "Hello, Noela. How is the petition coming along?"

"Wow, it's just amazing." Noela giggled with delight. "Two of us went around and we got over a hundred names each. I also told them about your mysterious stranger. Most of them took it as a good thing and signed the petition. I think we'll be able to overthrow that bylaw. We're planning activities for the youth here so they have something to do in the evenings. Maybe also push for Bible studies in the school. They're picking up so much garbage on the Internet."

"That is amazing! Carl did a good job writing out that petition. I'll tell him the good news. That Bible study is a good thing. Good work, Noela."

"Yes, tell him. Give him our thanks," Noela said.

"All right then, be talking to you." Kate hung up.

Carl, who was listening as he sat in front of the TV, was smiling. "Petition is doing well, I see."

"Yes, over a hundred signatures on each of them."

Carl said, "I smell frying fish. Man, do I ever want some fish for supper!" He got up from the couch and put on his parka. "I'm going across to ask Fred if he knows if anyone has been ice fishing. I'm going to buy a couple of pickerel." He strode out the door. "You can come, since you're carrying cash."

Kate slipped on her jacket and went out, grabbing her purse.

They approached Fred's house and heard agitated voices. Carl knocked, and Fred's loud voice said, "Come in."

Upon walking in they were greeted by a shaken Fred. He said, "Something happened to one of my kids. He's not breathing. Beverley called the ambulance."

Carl and Kate quickly went into the dining room. Beverley was screaming, "Please, God, don't take him now!"

On the floor lay their eight-year-old son, who was turning purple from lack of oxygen. Beverley was clutching him and sobbing. Her face was turned toward heaven, and tears were streaming down her face.

"Have you tried the Heimlich maneuver?" asked Carl.

"No. I hit his back to push out whatever was choking him, and then his eyes were rolling up," Fred said.

"I'll try it on him," Carl said as he straddled the boy. With his fist on his abdomen he thrust it upward and toward the esophagus. He kept doing the abdominal thrusts until the boy started to cough.

Carl quickly rolled him onto his side. Opening the child's mouth he poked his finger in and pulled out a piece of meat.

Throughout this entire time Kate was transfixed by Carl's unusual display of expertise. She realized Carl had hidden knowledge he'd never even discussed with her. She was relieved the boy was all right but felt left out of something she should have known.

She knew Carl did a lot of reading and watched TV. Admiration for her husband took over as he helped the boy.

Relief flooded Kate and the parents, but the boy seemed to lapse back into unconsciousness. "Do you want to do CPR on him, Kate?" asked Carl.

He tilted back the boy's head. Kate started breathing into the boy's mouth. Then she'd push down on his chest a few times and start the procedure over again. His eyes fluttered.

"Your turn," Kate said. Carl took over. The boy's colour was returning to normal. He seemed to breathing on his own, and he stirred.

They heard the siren of the ambulance coming in the distance and stopping outside. Beverley ran to the door and ushered the paramedics into the living room.

Fred told them, "Carl got a piece of meat out of him, and they tried CPR on him."

The paramedics examined him. With a stethoscope one listened to the boy's heart. The other one held a mirror to his mouth. He took his temperature, marking down their recordings.

"He's all right, but we'll take him in for observation. The doctor will give clearance and probably send him home after he examines him."

They went out and came back with a stretcher. They unfolded it and eased the semiconscious boy onto it. Covering him with a blanket, they carried him out and left.

"I'll go with him," Fred said. "Thanks, Carl. You saved my boy's life."

Carl smiled and gave him a wave.

"I'm coming," Beverley said. "My mother's on her way to sit with the kids." She closed the cellphone and thrust it into her pocket.

"I can wait here until she gets here," Kate said.

"Okay, thanks," the woman said as she slipped on her parka and winter boots.

Kate took off her jacket and sat down and yanked off her boots.

Carl said, "I'll go and sit with the kids, not that they really need me. It's funny—I don't really want fish anymore." He stepped out the door.

"See you shortly." Kate went into the bedroom to see the wide-eyed children sitting on their beds. Tears were rolling down the youngest one's face.

"Your grandma will be here in a little while," Kate said as she smiled to reassure them.

The older girl spoke up. "Is Bobby going to be all right?"

"He's breathing. That's a very good sign," Kate said.

"We were praying hard for him," the girl answered.

Kate realized she hadn't. She had been transfixed by the near casualty and had held her breath as they worked on Bobby. She felt disappointed in her lack of spirituality in a moment of crisis and humbled by her discovery that she wasn't entirely God-conscious. She was also happily aware that all ill feeling between her and Beverley and her kids was gone. Bobby's near-death had removed all that, and the future lay clear and unmarred with strife. For that she was grateful.

She said, "If you're not going to finish up your supper, I'll clear the table. If you want to, come and sit in the kitchen and talk come with me."

The children followed her into the kitchen, and one of them sat down to eat his meal.

Kate and the older girl were washing dishes when the grandmother walked in.

"Thanks, Kate. You can leave now," the elderly woman said, smiling appreciatively.

chapter ten

Kate was at work the next day. One of the teachers stopped to talk to her in the hallway.

"Did you hear that Angela gave her notice? She says she has to look after her mom, who's ailing."

"No, I haven't really spoken to her in a week," Kate responded. She secretly wondered if it had anything to do with the bad news the reps had given at the meeting.

"The road sure is slippery near the intersection. I actually slipped through it. It scared the day lights out me," the woman said.

"Yes, I know. Our tires are old, and that road isn't good for anyone," Kate said.

"If they don't salt that spot soon, there's going to be an accident there."

"I sure hope not."

Kate stayed in after school to correct papers and prepare for the next day. She heard a siren in the distance, and it seemed to go out of town. She wondered, but Carl would soon pick her up, and she shuffled the last few papers and put them away in her desk.

An uneasy felling settled over her as she went down the hall. Shadows seem to amplify the feeling of dread. Hoping to see Carl in the hallway, she peered into the entrance area, looking for his tall frame to appear. As she neared it to go to the parking lot, she craned her neck to look for their vehicle. A cold shiver ran through her. Not seeing it, she ran through the doors, scanning the parking lot and the road for their white Lumina. It was nowhere in sight.

Just then the band constable's truck came into view and turned into the parking lot. Her heart dropped as they pulled up beside her. They both got out. Kate's mouth went dry. *Oh, no! Something is terribly wrong*, she thought.

One of them said, "I'm sorry, but Carl has been in an accident just out of town, near where they started construction on the road this week. He couldn't stop in time when a front loader turned suddenly. Low white cars are hard to see in the winter."

Kate stared at them in disbelief. "He's supposed to pick me about now." Her voice came out laboured.

"Yes, we know. That's why we're here. We'll take you to the hospital to see him."

"Yes, okay," Kate said hoarsely, feeling numbness come over her. "I think I'm in shock." She climbed in to the back.

"How is he? Is he alive?" Kate asked, trying to maintain some composure. Her heart was beating in a strange way. It flipped and seemed to skip a beat. She grabbed herself in the chest and felt her breath leaving her.

"He's unconscious. We don't know the extent of his injuries," the constable replied.

Kate gasped for breath. Everything turned black.

Then she was standing in a beautiful meadow. She saw Carl standing in the dark-green lush grass dotted with purple and magenta flowers. Relief flooded her, and she felt happy. There was a peaceful atmosphere, and Carl was smiling, with the sun beaming down on him. She yelled out his name. The scene drifted away, and she heard voices but couldn't make sense of what they were saying. Then she heard a shrill siren above her.

She felt a cold blast of air, and she regained consciousness. She realized she was back in a world of pain.

"Oh no, Carl," she sobbed.

They had opened the windows, and she was lying on her side in the back. Something had been tucked under her head. They were travelling on the road. She let out a gut-wrenching cry.

Soon they were at the hospital, and there was an attendant at the door with a wheelchair ready to wheel her in. The constables helped her out to escort her to the chair, but Kate declined their offer, saying, "I'm sure I can walk. Thanks."

"They just wheeled him in a couple of minutes ago."

Kate brushed past them. She rushed into the emergency room.

The paramedics were moving Carl onto the examination table. The doctor immediately opened Carl's eyes and shone a light into them. One nurse unwrapped a sterilized bundle on a tray and arranged the contents.

Another nurse was taking his pulse. Then she grabbed a swab and sprayed it with an antiseptic solution. She started to clean his face.

The doctor said, "Get the ventilator. We're going to do an endotracheal intubation. Hurry."

The nurse rushed out and returned, pushing a machine from the next room.

The doctor said, "Give me the laryngoscope." He turned around and said to Kate, "I'm sorry, but you'll have to wait in the waiting room. We'll let you know when we're done and you can come in and see him."

Kate went out into the hall and sat down on a beige cushioned chair. She was thankful that the doctor was looking after him. She started to pray and then remembered that she hadn't called anyone.

She phoned Edna. "Carl is in the emergency room. He was in an accident."

"Oh, no! I'll be right there."

"The kids don't know. Can you bring them? Our car is demolished."

"Yes, of course."

Kate settled down into the chair again and dug into her purse. She pulled out the white pouch her mother had given her a long time ago. It contained a white rosary. She unraveled it and straightened the beads out. Before she'd pray she would phone her sister Noela and tell her.

"Noela, Carl is in the hospital, unconscious. He was in a car accident. Can you pray for him and ask your friends to pray, please?"

"Oh no! Carl is in the hospital?" repeated Noela. 'Yes, Kate, I'll do that right away."

Kate hung up, made the sign of the cross, and started her rosary. "I believe in God the Father Almighty, Creator of heaven and earth." She stopped. It was really hard to pray, to focus on praying. "I believe in Jesus Christ, his only Son, our Lord, who was conceived by the Holy Ghost, born of the Virgin Mary." Kate tried fervently to pray. She started to cry softly. "God, it's so hard to pray. So sorry, but all I can think of is Carl lying lifeless in there. He's in your hands, Lord."

She wiped her face and started again. She felt peace settle on her as she continued. She was oblivious of anyone who walked by, so deep was her praying.

She was finished the rosary when she felt a hand on her

shoulder. She looked up and saw Rose beside her. Even Issy was there and his brother Rob. Edna was coming in with the children.

Molly, Myra, and Tim ran toward their mother and wrapped their arms around her. They started crying quietly. They had kept everything pent up and released their fears in tears with her.

"How is he, Mom?" Molly asked tearfully.

"The doctor and nurses are working on him right now," Kate reassured them. "We can go and see him when they're done."

Kate held her children for a while and rocked Tim gently afterward. Tim seemed to be a state of shock, he was so quiet.

To her surprise, Beverly and Fred walked in.

"Bobby's home. He recovered shortly after he got here last night," Beverly said.

"We heard about Carl, and we wanted to come and spend some time with you and the kids," Fred said.

They came and gave her a hug. They went to sit down by Edna.

Rose came and sat down beside her and the kids.

"I happened to be walking to the store when I noticed the ambulance going by. I saw the constables going to the school. Then someone walked into the store and said they saw your smashed car at the construction site. The area is cordoned off by yellow tape, and the police are there. I hired someone to drive us here."

Kate hugged Rose and said, "I appreciate that very much. It is so good to have friends at a time like this."

Rose, who was prone to crying these days, wiped a tear off her face and said, "You were there for us, more than once."

"What are friends for?" Kate said, thankful that they were there.

"Oh yeah. Guess what?" Rose said as she sniffed. She broke into a smile and continued, "I'm so grateful that someone offered their house for us to keep for the winter. They are moving out to take training at the Red River Community College."

"That's wonderful," Kate said.

The nurse came out. She announced with a kind smile, "You can come and see him briefly, and only a few people at a time. He's resting, and we're keeping a close eye on him, monitoring his progress."

Kate took her children in first to see their father, who was hooked up to the ventilator. He had been cleaned and a clean hospital gown put on him. He lay under his white sheet looking like he was sleeping. The children kissed him.

"We love you, Daddy," Myra said.

"Dad, I'm not playing hockey until you come home," Tim said. "I'll be waiting for you."

Molly stroked his hand as it lay limp beside him. "Good night, Dad," she said and left the room.

Edna came in, and Myra went out to join Molly, but Tim stayed beside Carl.

Edna gazed at Carl and felt his forehead. She felt his hand for a pulse. She frowned and said, "I can't feel a pulse."

The nurse came over and examined Carl. She listened with her stethoscope and nodded.

"Yes, there is one." She smiled at Edna reassuringly. Relief flooded Edna's face.

"I'm a bigger worrier than you. I should have more faith. His relatives will probably be here too. His sisters will be arriving in town by morning to come and visit him."

The nurse said quietly, "Okay, let him rest for a while. We'll be wheeling him into a room in the ICU unit."

They all filed out and sat down.

Jeremy walked in with a box filled with coffee and water bottles. He said to them, "I thought you might want something to drink." He handed all the adults a cup of coffee and the children the bottles of water.

"How is Carl?" he asked.

"He's resting, and they're keeping a close eye on him," Edna said.

Jeremy sat down, and everyone drank their coffee in silence.

"I phoned Noela in Mossy Point and asked her to ask her friends to pray for Carl. I forgot to phone the people from the church," Kate said.

"Don't worry about them. I'll call a couple of them now," Edna said. She went to the pay phone.

After she got off the phone, Edna said, "I'll take the kids home to feed them. We'll come back after. We'll bring you some sandwiches."

Kate nodded.

"I better take the boys back, too, and feed them," Rose said. "I'll try to come back later too."

"I'll stay for a while," Jeremy said.

chapter eleven

Kate and Jeremy kept their vigil in the visitor's lounge for the next two hours. Every little while, Kate would go in to see Carl. The nurse hooked Carl up to an IV and then left.

Jeremy went in a couple of times. Finally Jeremy said, "I'll go and get the children if you want. And I'll check on your sandwich."

Just then, the priest from Kate's church walked in. Father James was an old man with a grey beard, and he carried a little black bag. "Edna phoned me and asked if I'd come and minister the anointing of the sick to Carl," he said. "She'll be here shortly with the children."

"Of course. Come with me," Kate said. "I'm so glad she phoned you. I didn't even think of doing that."

"I'll need a cart or table to use as an altar," he said.

"I'll go and ask the nurses at the desk," Jeremy said and was out the door.

Kate moved the chair back from the bed. Jeremy returned with a cart a few minutes later and wheeled it inside the room.

Edna and the children could be heard coming down the hallway as Father James unpacked his little bag and laid out a white cloth on the cart. He set out his book of vespers and his Bible, bottles of holy water and oil. He put on a stole around his neck and then his chasuble, a white vestment. He made the sign of the cross and sprinkled holy water around and blessed the premises.

Father James began by praying. He read portions of Psalm 16 and a passage from James 5 about anointing of the sick. Then he gave a short litany about the readings. He whispered prayers for forgiveness of Carl's sins and then applied oil on Carl's forehead.

He prayed, "Through this anointing may the Lord in his love and mercy help you with grace of his Holy Spirit."

He anointed Carl's hands and said, "May the Lord who frees you from sin save you and raise you up."

Everyone murmured, "Amen."

Father James took his prayer book and read some prayers for the sick. He performed the transubstantiation and gave everyone in the room the holy Eucharist. He finished with a prayer of blessing and peace on everyone. Then he folded up all his white clothes and placed everything inside his bag.

Everyone thanked him for coming before he left.

Edna was holding a brown paper bag all this time. Molly opened up the bag and pulled out a sandwich and a drink for Kate.

Then Molly handed the bag to Jeremy. "There's one for you, too."

"I'll be sleeping here tonight," Kate said, "probably on that chair, so you can sleep over at your grandma's." Turning to Edna she said, "Unless you want to keep them at our house."

"I'll let them decide where they want to sleep," Edna replied.

After a couple of hours, when the children were starting to fall asleep, Edna woke them up and took them home. It was quiet after everyone left. The machine was the only thing that gave light in the dark room as Kate sat huddled in the chair beside Carl's bed. Once in while she'd stroke his head or his hand or kiss his forehead.

Every so often the nurse would come in to monitor the equipment and take Carl's vital signs. She'd check his catheter before leaving. She brought a cup of coffee for Kate during one of her visits. Kate sat sipping her coffee, watching his breathing.

She left once to use the bathroom. When she returned, it seemed that Carl's hand had moved from his side to his thigh. *I must have moved it there myself*, she thought.

The only prayer she murmured throughout the night was "God, heal Carl, please."

In the wee hours of the night Kate nodded off from sheer exhaustion, with her head falling forward. She slept for a full hour. She was in that position when the nurse walked in to check on Carl. When the nurse moved the ventilator, Kate woke up. She saw the nurse make adjustments on it.

"What's happening?" Kate asked.

"I'm changing the air flow from assist control to intermittent mandatory ventilation."

"Is that good?" Kate asked anxiously.

"Yes. His vital signs have improved, and he'll breathe with less help. I'm going to get the doctor to come and check him again." She left.

"Did you hear that, Carl?" Kate said as she gave his hand a squeeze. "I'm going to phone and tell your mom and the kids." She walked out to the hall and called Edna.

"Hello," answered Edna. "How is he?"

"His vital signs improved, and he's getting less help to breathe from the machine."

"That's wonderful! I'll see you shortly."

The doctor and nurse were walking into the ICU unit when Kate went back to Carl's room. She decided to wait outside by the door. She felt refreshed by hope and was wide awake. She noticed it was almost four o'clock and made a mental note to phone the principal as soon as possible to let him know she wouldn't be at work.

The doctor was smiling when they came out. "He has some bruising to this lung. We're going to keep on the ventilator for a while until I'm confident he can breathe easy without it. He's conscious. You can see him for a few minutes, but you'll have to let him rest. His body has taken a beating."

Kate was beside herself with joy. She went in and rushed to his bedside.

Carl was awake. He smiled weakly.

Kate kissed him. Tears of joy glistened in her eyes. "I'm so relieved," she whispered. "I was so scared we'd lost you." She took Carl's hand, and he gave it a little squeeze.

"Your mom is coming. I let her know as soon as the nurse said you were improving."

The nurse walked in and said, "Okay, I'm afraid you'll have to let him rest now."

Kate said as she was leaving the room, "I'll be out here waiting."

Edna arrived not long after. Kate told her, "He opened his eyes, and he recognized me. It could have been worse. He could have had amnesia."

Edna went in to see Carl. Kate followed her.

Carl had fallen back into sleep. They stood staring at him for a few minutes and then left.

"Let's go and have something to eat. I think we can get something from the kitchen downstairs," Edna said. They went down the stairwell and asked the cook for coffee and some toast, then sat down and ate.

Kate said, "You know, the passenger we picked up over the weekend left his knapsack behind in the back seat of our car.

We couldn't locate him, so we looked in it and found a Bible with a note saying to use it, so Carl has been reading that Bible all week."

"Yes, he told me about the mystery man on the road. You both forgot the name of the city he was heading for?"

"We only remember his name."

"What was his name?"

"Christianson is all I remember now. Maybe it'll come to me later."

Carl was waking up when they went back into the ICU unit. They both went to kiss him.

He slept on and off for the rest of the day, but he seemed to get better and stronger as the day went on.

They removed the ventilator in the afternoon but kept his IV in.

The next day Carl was able to talk. He started his story. "I was in a beautiful land, and I met someone in white who told me I couldn't stay. I had to go back and finish the work I'm supposed to do. I have to teach my children about God. It was such a wonderful place, I hated leaving. I'm sorry, but although I love you I wanted to stay there. I agreed to come back because I knew you would be too hurt if I stayed. I have much to teach my children and whoever will listen."

"Yes, you do. And I'm glad you decided to come back." Kate kissed him ever so gently on the lips.

CPSIA information can be obtained at www.ICGtesting.com
Printed in the USA
LVOW04s0351070215

426049LV00011B/89/P

9 781486 604685